Here Comes Mr. Dragon!

Based on the television episodes
"Dragon Boat Festival," by Sascha Paladino,
and "Hoho's Big Flight," by Adam Peltzman
Illustrated by A&J Studios

A GOLDEN BOOK • NEW YORK

ISBN: 978-0-375-85106-3
www.randomhouse.com/kids
Printed in the United States of America
10 9 8 7 6 5 4 3 2 1

Ni hao! That's how I say *hello* in Chinese!

Mr. Sun is sleeping. We'd better wake him up!

I know! We can tickle him. Stretch out your arms, wiggle your fingers, and tickle, tickle!

Circle the Mr. Sun who is awake.

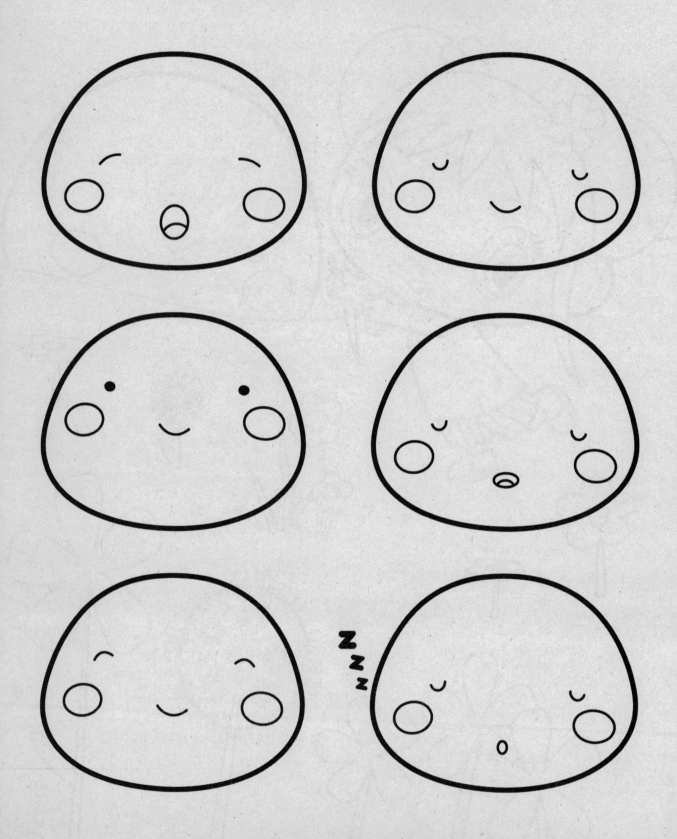

Today is the Dragon Boat Festival!

We get to race dragon boats and do dragon dances.

And after the race, we get to meet Mr. Dragon!

I drew a picture to give to Mr. Dragon.
Do you think he'll like it?

Have you ever met a dragon?
Draw one here.

My grandfather, YeYe, is making a dragon boat. Help him decorate it.

"Tiger, tiger, ROAR!"

It's our friend Rintoo the tiger.
He can't wait for the race!

Everyone can do my dragon dance!
Let's do the dragon dance together!

Jump up like a dragon.

Crouch like a dragon.

Wiggle like a dragon.

Flap like a dragon.

Super dragon dancing!

Our friends Hoho and Tolee want to dragon dance with us, too!

Look! It's Lulu and Howard!
Ni men hao! Hello, you two!

We're all going to the Dragon Boat Festival.
There it is!

"I have my special racing helmet
and my floaty jacket!"

**The Peeking Mouse's drum
will tell us how fast to paddle.**

Let's go, go, go!

Rintoo, we have to paddle together.

Look! Lulu and Hoho are out in front.
Help them get to the Red Bridge to win the race!

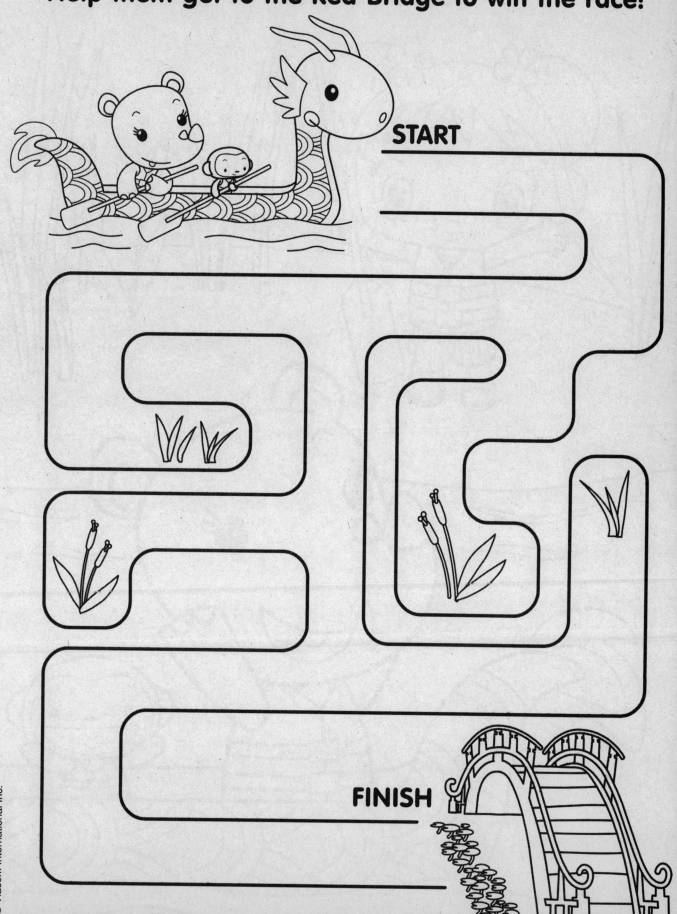

START

FINISH

Lulu and Hoho have won the race!
Super! *Tai hao le!*

Everybody is happy but Rintoo! Draw an angry face on him.

"We lost the race! It's not fair!"

"Kai-lan, why did Rintoo kick the boat up there?"

I don't know.
Do you think Rintoo is mad because we lost the race?

"I'm mad, mad, mad!
And I don't want to race anymore."

"But if Rintoo isn't in the next race,
he'll never meet Mr. Dragon!"

YeYe, what can we do to help Rintoo?

"It's hard to do anything when we're mad.
Rintoo has to calm down."

Look at Hoho. He's pretty calm.

**Hoho is calm because he's swaying
with the Hula Ducks.
Draw yourself dancing with them.**

Now Rintoo is swaying with the Hula Ducks, too. Does he still look mad?

It's okay to feel mad, Rintoo.
But then we have to calm down.

How will we get the dragon boat down?

I know! Hoho is a great jumper.
To help him jump up to get the boat, say *"Tiao!"*

Super job, Hoho!
Now let's row together, Rintoo.

Trace the lines and finish the paddles for Kai-lan and Rintoo.

Hooray! We rowed together, and we won!

This is where Mr. Dragon lives.
We can do the dragon dance to call him.

Ni hao, Mr. Dragon!

"Kai-lan, I'm glad I calmed down and we all got to see Mr. Dragon."

I gave Mr. Dragon the dragon picture I drew.
Do you think he likes it?

Look at the pretty flower that Mr. Dragon left us!

Let's give the pretty flower to YeYe.
Will you color it for him?

KEY
1=PINK 2=YELLOW 3=GREEN

"I have the perfect place for this flower, Kai-lan."

I'm so glad you were here to help us.
You make my heart feel super happy. *Zai jian!*

Ni hao!
I'm excited because tonight
I get to stay up late!

LANTERN
FESTIVAL

**Tonight is the Lantern Festival.
My friends and family carry lanterns around
in the dark. I love the Lantern Festival!**

The wind is blowing my hair—and YeYe's lantern!

Circle YeYe's lantern. It's the one that's different.

Don't worry, YeYe! I got it!

**"That was a really good catch.
Thank you, Kai-lan. *Xie xie!*"**

YeYe has lots of lanterns for the Lantern Festival. Draw lines to connect the ones that match.

I have an idea! We can get all our friends to paint animals on the lanterns. See you later, YeYe!

I hear something!
The Chinese word for *listen* is *ting*.
Let's listen together. Say *"Ting!"*

It's Rintoo!

"I want to decorate the lanterns, too! I love lanterns!"

Hoho, do you want to paint lanterns with us?

Hoho is not listening to us.

It's time to choose a lantern to paint.
Follow the path to see which one Tolee chooses.

START

Hoho didn't pick a lantern.
Do you think he's listening to us?

"I'm going to paint a dragon on my lantern!"

What animal do you want on your lantern? Draw it here.

Look! The Peeking Mice are getting ready
to play music at the Lantern Festival.
It's almost festival time!

"It's very, very windy!
Make sure your lanterns don't blow away."

Oh, no! Hoho's lantern is blowing away because he didn't listen to YeYe!

Hoho caught his lantern—
but now he's blowing away with it!

We have to find Hoho! Do you see him?

We have to save Hoho before he blows away! Help us find the path that leads to him.

FINISH

START

"I've got him!"

"It's very windy. If we put apples on our lanterns,
they won't blow away."

"This apple looks yummy! I think I'll eat it."

"Look! Hoho's lantern blew away again!"

"Hoho's lantern flew away because he didn't put his apple on it."

Why didn't Hoho put an apple on his lantern?
Do you think he was listening to YeYe?

"I'm sorry I wasn't listening."

That's okay, Hoho. We're going to help you listen, because you're our friend.

Do you know who are really good listeners? The Peeking Mice.

"First we use our ears to listen! *Ting!*"

Do you think Hoho should listen carefully and look at whoever is talking? I think so, too! WE GOT IT!

YeYe tells everyone to line up for the Lantern Festival. Do you think Hoho is listening?

"I wasn't listening, Kai-lan,
but I know just what to do!"

"I put my hand to my ear.
That helps me to hear! *Ting!*"

"I use my eyes to see
who's talking to me.
Listen! Listen! Listen! *Ting!*"

Help us find Hoho's lantern.
Circle the one with a monkey on it.

"Hoho has his lantern,
but now it's getting really dark."

Excuse me, fireflies.
Would you please light our lanterns?

"The glowing lanterns mean good luck for all of us!"

"Thanks for helping me, Kai-lan! I love you!"

This is the best Lantern Festival ever!

**Thank you for all your help!
You make my heart feel super happy! *Zai jian!***